George Ancona

BANANAS

FROM MANOLO TO MARGIE

CLARION BOOKS
TICKNOR & FIELDS : A HOUGHTON MIFFLIN COMPANY : NEW YORK

To Tomaz Farkas, *amigo.*

CLARION BOOKS
Ticknor & Fields, a Houghton Mifflin Company

Designed by George Ancona

Library of Congress Cataloging in Publication Data

Ancona, George.
Bananas: from Manolo to Margie.

Summary: Follows the journey of a banana from Honduras where it is grown to North
America where it is eventually consumed.
1. Banana—Juvenile literature. [1. Banana]   I. Title.

SB379.B2A46	641.3′4772	82-1247
ISBN 0-89919-100-2		AACR2

Meet Manolo.

   His real name is Manuel, the same as his father's. To tell the difference, his family calls him by his nickname, Manolo.

Manolo lives on a banana plantation in Honduras, one of the countries of Central America. Here the climate is tropical, and the hot, humid, rainy weather is just right to grow bananas.

More than five hundred years ago, the Portuguese discovered bananas in Africa. They took some plants to the Canary Islands along with their African name. From there a Spanish missionary carried banana roots to the New World and planted them. Soon bananas were growing in many of the lands surrounding the Caribbean Sea. Today, Central America exports two-thirds of the world's bananas.

Manolo's father, Señor Velez, is a *bananero*, a farm worker who cares for banana plants. He works on a *finca*, or plantation, owned by a fruit company.

Tropical rains often cause flooding, so the house the family lives in is built on stilts. The open area below is used as a living room. Hammocks are hung there for cool *siestas*, or naps. Here Manolo lives with his father, mother, sister, brother, and pet parrot, which speaks Spanish as everyone in Honduras does.

Bananas grow on tall plants. They are not trees because neither their trunks nor the roots are woody. The plant grows from a bulb called a rhizome, and it is a perennial, which means it grows from the same rhizome year after year. Most plants stand anywhere from eight to sixteen feet (2.4 to 4.8 m) tall. Their huge leaves are over six feet (1.8 m) long and more than a foot (30.5 cm) wide.

The plant grows very fast, often as much as an inch (2.5 cm) or more each night. Some people say that if you stand very still after a rain you can hear the plants sighing from their growing pains.

In eight or nine months the plant is fully grown. This is called the mother plant. At its base, other, younger plants are growing from the same rhizome. These are the future generations of daughter and granddaughter plants, which will bear fruit.

1. Up through the center of the plant grows a thick stem with a large bud at the end. It comes out of the top of the plant and arches down. This is a two-day-old bud. It is covered with purple leaves called bracts.

2. In about nine days the bracts on the stem roll back to reveal rows of flowers. Each row will become a "hand" of bananas. Each hand has from ten to twenty "fingers," or bananas, on it.

3. The tiny bananas first grow down, then out, and finally up.

4. In ninety days the fruit is ready to be cut down. Each stem has about 150 bananas and can weigh up to 100 pounds (45.36 kg). Only one stem will be produced by each banana plant.

On some days Manolo's father works as a *protejedor* or protector of the plants.

First he cuts off the tip of the bud. He saves this to show how many plants he protected that day. Then he removes the entire bud so that all the plant's energy will go into the fruit.

Next Señor Velez covers the fruit with a polyethylene bag to keep out insects. He then ties on a colored plastic ribbon. Different colors indicate when the fruit will be ready to harvest. To prevent winds and the weight of the fruit from toppling the plant, Señor Velez ties each plant to the bases of neighboring plants.

At the end of the day, Señor Velez sets out the tips for the foreman to count. He is paid according to the number of plants he took care of.

Early each weekday morning Manolo, his
sister, and other children of the finca
walk to the nearby rural school. Many of
the girls carry parasols to protect them
from the hot sun. The boys wear white
shirts and the girls wear white dresses.
During their geography lesson Manolo
learns about foreign lands like the
United States.

Thousands of miles away, the markets need bananas. The company's headquarters telegraphs the finca with the order to cut fruit.

Now Señor Velez straps on his *machete* and goes to work as a *cortero*, or cutter. His friend José works with him as a *juntero*, the gatherer of fruit. José wears a pad on his shoulder to protect the fruit from bruising while he carries it.

For the best flavor, bananas must be harvested green, then allowed to ripen. The fruit is measured, and when the right size is found, Señor Velez nicks the stalk of the plant. This lowers the fruit onto José's shoulder. Then with one blow of his machete Señor Velez cuts through the stem, and the fruit drops.

While José carries the fruit away, Señor Velez cuts down the rest of the mother plant. This will fertilize the daughter and granddaughter plants.

A network of cables carries the green bananas from every corner of the finca to the packing plant. After a row of stems is hung on the cable, a man driving a tiny engine hooks up to it. Here begins the first leg of the fruit's long journey north. In about two weeks these bananas will be in a foreign store, ripe, yellow, and ready to eat.

After work, the bananeros enjoy a fast game of soccer. Teams are formed between workers from different sections of the finca. Manolo and his friends choose sides and have their own bare-foot game of soccer.

Dinnertime in the Velez kitchen gives the family a chance to compare the events of the day. As part of their meals, people in Honduras eat *tortillas*, the Indian bread made of ground corn.

Inside the packing plant, a worker stands at the end of each cable and cuts the bananas off the stems. He separates the smaller fruit, which will be made into baby food and flavorings. The larger fruit he puts into a huge tank of running water. The water carries the fruit to a row of women standing at the other end of the tank. They wash the fruit and discard any bruised ones.

The best bananas go into another tank, which carries the fruit to a group of women, who weigh it.

Standing at a scale, each woman fills a
tray with forty pounds (18.14 kg) of
bananas. The trays are then pushed
down a conveyor to another woman,
who packs the fruit into cartons.

Manolo's mother, Señora Velez, works
as a packer. She wraps the fruit in heavy
paper to protect it, covers the box, and
the bananas are on their way to market.

The cartons move along a conveyor to a waiting railroad boxcar. The men inside the boxcar will load nine hundred boxes of fruit into each car.

Sometimes Manolo and his father walk down to the packing plant to meet Señora Velez. While waiting for her, they often talk to the engineer who picks up the boxcars. The diesel engine will gather more cars from all the packing plants and take them to the seaport. And so the bananas that the Velez family and their neighbors have planted, protected, harvested, carried, sorted, washed, weighed, and packed are on their way to distant markets and unknown people.

Two and a half hours later, after traveling through the lush Honduran country-side, the train arrives at the seaport. There it meets the waiting reefer. Reefers are refrigerated ships designed and built to keep their cargoes cool. They are insulated and painted white to reflect the heat of the tropical sun. The ships are at sea for months at a time, picking up and delivering perishable cargoes all over the world.

Longshoremen roll open the doors of the boxcars. Straight and curved sections of roller conveyors are connected together. These carry the boxes from the boxcars to the ship-loading gantries.

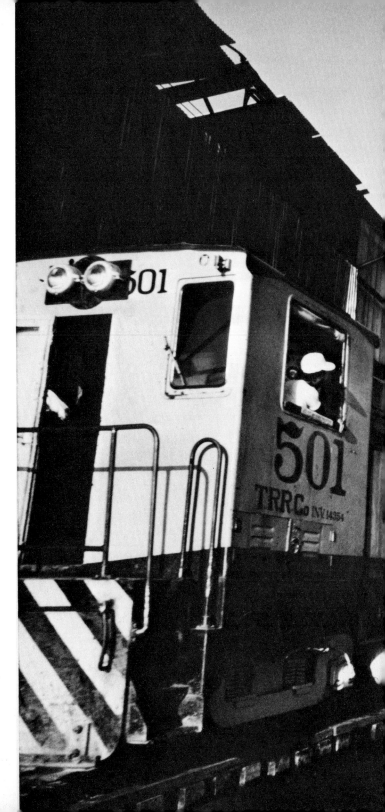

At the rate of four boxes a second, these gantries lift the boxes off the dock and carry them up, over, and into the hold of the ship.

On the dock some of the boxes are opened by an inspector to check the quality of the fruit. He takes the temperature of the bananas with a thermometer. Once cut, the bananas must stay green until they reach market. The reefer will cool the fruit to 56°–58°F (13°–14°C) to keep it from ripening.

Below deck the longshoremen work through the night. To fill the ship they will load 275,000 boxes of bananas.

As dawn comes, the first officer prepares to get the ship under way. He checks all the electronics and communication systems. After the conveyors are raised and the hatches closed, the captain gives the order to cast off. The sleek white reefer is on her way to one of the big cities of the world. It's the captain's job to make sure the bananas don't ripen at sea. To prevent this, the temperature of the fruit is checked constantly.

When the ship arrives close to its destination, a small pilot boat comes from shore to greet it. A rope ladder is thrown over the side of the ship and a person called a pilot climbs aboard. From now until the ship is safe at the dock, the pilot will navigate through all the twists and turns of the harbor and river.

Early the next morning the hatches are opened and the gantries lower their conveyors into the hold. Longshoremen come aboard and go below deck to begin unloading. It will take two days to unload the ship.

As the boxes leave the gantries, they roll out on conveyors to the rows of waiting refrigerator trucks. These trucks continue to keep the bananas at the right temperature for the rest of their trip. The trucks will fan out to many distant cities with their cargoes of green bananas. The drivers are at the wheel for many hours. Some of these trucks have cabs that are large enough to sleep in when the driver pulls into a rest stop.

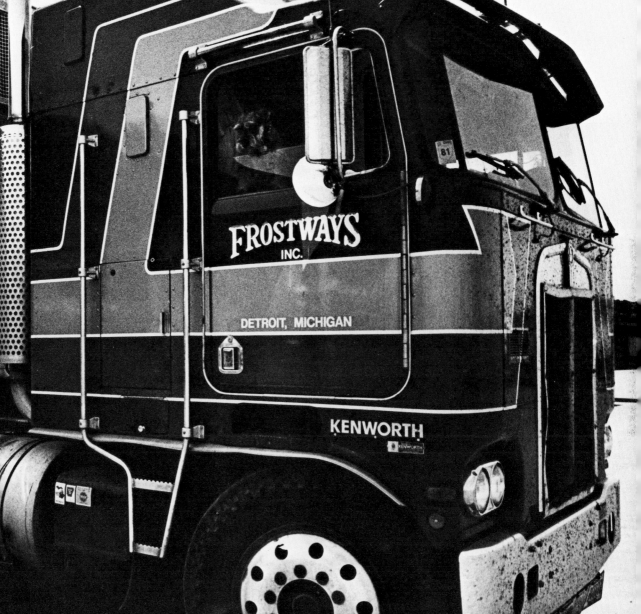

Each city has a wholesale market where produce comes in from farms to be sold to retail storekeepers. Here owners of stores both big and small come to buy the many fruits and vegetables they will sell to their customers.

Trucks carrying bananas are quickly unloaded, and boxes are stacked on a wooden platform called a pallet. A power jack lifts each pallet and rolls it into a ripening room. A forklift will stack the boxes until the room is filled.

As fruits ripen, they give off heat and ethylene gas naturally. To trigger the ripening process and make sure all the bananas ripen together, the wholesaler releases ethylene gas in the ripening room. Now the dealer can regulate the time it will take to ripen the bananas.

Inside the cartons the bananas begin to change from solid green to yellow. The hard fruit softens and becomes sweet as its starches change to fructose. In four or five days, only the tips have a touch of green. Now the bananas are ready to be sold to the grocer.

Most people buy bananas
when only the tips are green.

From midnight to early morning, while most people are asleep, the wholesale market is a bustle of activity. Trains and trucks roll in and out, workers shout and toot their forklift horns as they unload the trucks, and retailers bargain with wholesale merchants.

A retailer is a person who sells directly to you, the customer. Retailers will buy as many cases of bananas as they expect to sell in their stores.

A storekeeper may bring his children to the market when they have a day off from school.

Margie and her mother shop at the corner store of Mr. and Mrs. Lu. There is always a colorful display of fruit in front of the store. Margie picks out a bunch of ripe bananas to buy.

Margie loves bananas. Since bananas
don't have to be washed, she eats one on
the way home. And while she eats she
thinks of the bananas' long journey. She
would like to say to all those people . . .

. . . thank you for the bananas.

A fully ripe banana, one with golden skin flecked with brown spots, has the sweetest taste. It is easy to digest and gives us many nutrients our bodies need. When you eat 100 grams of banana, a medium-sized banana, this is what you get:

Water	75.7%
Food Energy	85 calories
Protein	1.1 g
Fat	0.2 g
Carbohydrates	22.2 g
Ash	.8 g
Vitamin A	190 IU
Thiamine (B_1)	0.05 mg
Riboflavin (B_2)	0.06 mg
Niacin	0.7 mg
Vitamin C	10 mg
Calcium	8 mg
Phosphorous	26 mg
Iron	0.7 mg
Sodium	1 mg
Potassium	370 mg

These figures from *Composition of Foods*, USDA Agricultural Handbook #8, Revised December 1963

GLOSSARY OF SPANISH WORDS

amigo (a MEE go) a friend

bananero (ban a NAIR o) a farm worker who cares for banana plants

cortero (kor TAIR o) the worker who cuts the stem of bananas from the plant

finca (FEEN ka) a farm or ranch, especially a large farm such as a plantation

juntero (hoon TAIR o) the worker who carries the stem of bananas on his shoulder

machete (ma CHE tay) a knife with a long, curved blade used for cutting plants

protejedor (pro TAY hey dor) the farm worker who protects the banana plants while they are growing

señor (sayn YOR) the title for a man, which is similar to the English *Mr.*

señora (sayn YOR a) the title for a married woman, which is similar to the English *Mrs.*

siesta (see ES ta) a nap during the heat of the day, usually after the midday meal

tortillas (tor TEE yas) flat bread made from cornmeal or flour

For their assistance and cooperation, which made this book possible, I should like to thank George Bobinski, George Eldridge, Nancy Ambrosino, Dennis Sullivan, Mike Ballinger, John Bishop, Thomas Pino, Don Morrison, and Robertin Turnbull, all of United Brands, Inc., the Velez family of Finca San Juan, Honduras, Jim Gabourel of the Tela Railroad Co., Captain Lockie and the officers and crew of the ship *Snow Storm*, Captain Backes and the officers and crew of the *Pocantico*, Martin and Jeff Striks, Mr. and Mrs. Lu of the Star Market, Paul Capel, Joe Budnick, Paul Carol, Margie and Kate Reuther.